SANTA'S LETTERS

Illustrated by JOHN BLACKMAN

Written by AMBER HUNT

TEMPLAR

"It's no good," said Santa loudly. "I'm getting too old for this."

It was nearly 25th December and Santa was terribly behind with Christmas.

He had been complaining for days that there were still hundreds of presents to make and thousands of letters to open.

"Nonsense," said Otter who helped Santa wrap the Christmas parcels. "You're magic, Santa, so you never age!"

"I know, I know," said Santa, "but that doesn't stop me *feeling* too old, does it? However am I going to get everything done in time?" But Otter just yawned and smiled a secret smile.

Just then Mouse appeared. She usually helped Santa tie ribbons round all the special gifts, but today she wasn't working because she had a winter cold.

"Atishoo," she squeaked. "Have you seen my handkerchief?"

"No, I haven't," said Santa crossly and he walked away reading yet another letter.

4

In the toy room Polar Bear had fallen fast asleep. He had been busy making teddy bears and had nodded off waiting for the glue to dry.

"Wake up! Wake up!" cried Santa. "Here's another request for a teddy bear and you haven't even finished yesterday's orders yet."

"Z z z z z," snored Polar Bear, who turned over and carried on sleeping.

"Well, really," said Santa, shaking his head. "Let's just hope we don't get any *more* letters asking for teddy bears today."

Just then there was a knock at the door. Otter opened it. It was the postman and can you guess what he had with him? Why, it was another HUGE sack — full of letters.

8

"At this rate I'll have to cancel Christmas altogether," said Santa glumly. And he went off to write another list of things to do.

9

"Atishoo," sneezed little Mouse, who was following Santa. "Have *you* seen my handkerchief," she inquired politely of the polar bear.

"Z z z z z z," snored Polar Bear helpfully.

"Well, really," said the mouse, and she searched all round the toy room to see if she could find it. But all she found were toys and letters, letters and toys, covering every available space.

"Never mind," said Mouse and she set off for the packing room to have a look there.

To Santa Claus
NORTHPOLE

To Santa
Snowland

To Santa Claus
Top of the World

Otter had gone to the packing room too. He was standing in the corner surrounded by a little group of animals, whispering intently.

"Watch out," cried Penguin suddenly. "Here comes Santa."

Sure enough, there was Santa trailing a great long list of new presents to be packed.

"We need four train sets, five jigsaws and sixteen talking dollies!" he cried. "And don't forget those teddy bears!"

13

Santa was so busy reading his list that he didn't even notice that the animals stopped talking together as soon as he came near. Nor did he see that as soon as his back was turned they started whispering again.

No, Santa's head was full of other things. For a start, he'd just opened a letter asking for a real live dinosaur and he had absolutely no idea where to find one of those...

To Santa NORWAY.

Back in the packing room there was the sound of sneezing.

"Please has anyone seen my handkerchief?" said Mouse as she searched amongst the piles of coloured paper. But the other animals were so busy whispering to each other that they didn't even hear her.

"Oh well," sighed Mouse and she set off to search the post room instead.

In the post room Santa was busy ticking off all the letters he had received against all the parcels that were ready to go out. There were parcels for children all over the world — parcels destined for children in Australia and Africa, parcels addressed to the South Pole and the North Pole and every other country in between.

And in each one was a lovely present just waiting to be opened.

To Jessica and Claudia
AUSTRALIA

Santa began to feel quite cheerful at the sight of all those parcels ready to be loaded onto his sleigh. Then he heard the sound of snoring. It was Badger.

Badger was in charge of the post room and he was supposed to be busy labelling the parcels as they came in from the packing room. But instead here he was asleep under his desk!

"Whatever next!" muttered Santa as he shook Badger awake. "Isn't anyone else worried that we're late for Christmas this year!"

The next day it was just the same. More letters arrived, and it was the same the day after that and the day after that. Poor Santa was so busy that he didn't know whether he was coming or going. And everywhere he went there seemed to be animals whispering in corners or, even worse, animals falling fast asleep.

Why, that very morning he had found Otter (who was usually most reliable) sound asleep in the postman's sack! The only person who seemed really busy was Mouse, but all she was doing was looking for her missing handkerchief.

And so Santa's list of letters got longer and longer. So long in fact that he was about to give up and take a job as a deckchair attendant somewhere nice and warm. But, just in time, Otter and the other animals came to see him.

To Santa Claus
Lapland

They dug Santa out from beneath his huge pile of paper and tied a colourful scarf around his eyes so that he couldn't see where he was going. Then they led him into the middle of the big workshop and sat him down in his favourite chair.

Santa couldn't believe his eyes when Polar Bear took the scarf away. For in front of him was the the biggest present he had ever seen. It was wrapped in red spotty paper and tied with a beautiful yellow bow.

"Go on, open it," the animals laughed. "It's your Christmas present Santa. But we thought it might help you if you opened it early..."

And so Santa opened it. And there it was — the cause of all the yawning and the whispering. The thing the animals had been making for weeks, mostly at night and always in secret — a magic Christmas computer.

"Look," said Polar Bear. "You put the letters in here and pictures of the presents come up on the screen. We make the presents and put them in here. Then the computer wraps and labels them and drops them into the sack here!"

"How marvellous!" said Santa. "All my problems are over. We need never be late for Christmas again."

"Atishoo," squeaked Mouse who was pointing excitedly at the computer screen.

"Isn't that my handkerchief?" she said.

And, of course, it was!